A catalogue record for this book is available from the British Library

Published by Ladybird Books Ltd
27 Wrights Lane London W8 5TZ
A Penguin Company

4 6 8 10 9 7 5

Printed in Italy

Disney's THE TIGGER MOVIE

Ladybird

One autumn day, Tigger was bouncing his way through the Hundred Acre Wood.

Bouncing was so much fun that Tigger wanted someone to share it. So he went to see Pooh.

"Wanna go bouncing?" Tigger cried.

"I can't," said Pooh. "I'm collecting honey for the winter."

When Tigger bounced on, he met Piglet. But Piglet was busy – preparing for winter.

Then Tigger thought of Roo. But only Kanga was at home – preparing for winter.

"What's all this winter busyness?" wondered Tigger, bouncing off.

Tigger didn't know it, but his happy bouncing had disturbed a big rock on the hill just above Eeyore's house. And that rock had rolled downhill, crushing poor Eeyore's home.

Of course, all Eeyore's friends came to help. They looked at the rock and wondered what to do.

Then up bounced Tigger. "Anyone up for a little bouncin'?" he asked.

"No!" said Rabbit. "No bouncing!" He pointed at the rock. "Can't you see we have to move this?"

Tigger helped in the only way he knew how. He bounced. And it worked! The rock fell down the rest of the hill, taking everyone with it.

"We did it!" cried Tigger, pleased. "*Now*, who's up for a little bouncing?"

The others looked at one another. "The thing is," said Piglet, "we can't bounce like you because…"

"…we're not Tiggers," finished Pooh.

So Tigger went off by himself, feeling very lonely.

Roo followed him. "Tigger," he said, "maybe you aren't alone. Maybe you have a family somewhere."

"Hey, a Tigger family! All bouncing together!" said Tigger excitedly.

Roo and Tigger went to ask Owl how to find Tigger's family.

"First you must find your family tree," said Owl wisely.

"My family tree!" exclaimed Tigger. "It's sure to be the most gigantical tree in the entire Wood. Let's go find it, Roo." So off they went.

Meanwhile, the others were helping Eeyore. But suddenly Tigger and Roo bounced past – right on top of Eeyore's rebuilt home. Tigger was calling, "Hey, where are you, Tigger family?"

When silence fell, Eeyore said, "Tigger seems to have lost his family."

"Should we help him to find them?" asked Pooh.

Tigger and Roo went on bouncing and looking, but with no luck. At last Tigger decided to go home.

When they got there, Tigger showed Roo the Whoop-de-Dooper Bounce.

Roo began bouncing to and fro. Then suddenly he knocked into Tigger's cupboard, and found a small locket. Tigger picked it up. "This should have a family portrait in it," he said, sighing. "Where are all those Tiggers?"

"Why don't you send them a letter?" suggested Roo.

So that's what Tigger did.

Meanwhile, Eeyore, Piglet and Pooh were also looking for Tigger's family. They soon found some bouncing, stripey creatures, but they weren't proper Tiggers.

Pooh climbed a tree and saw some more stripey creatures – but they were bees. Pooh, who loved honey, couldn't resist a quick mouthful or two. He sang the bees to sleep, then reached out his paw.

But it wasn't long before the bees awoke and chased the friends away.

Tigger and Roo were still waiting for a reply to Tigger's letter. But soon it began to snow, and Roo had to go home.

"I wish I had a big brother like Tigger," he told Kanga later that night.

"But Roo, Tigger is just like one of our family," said Kanga. That gave Roo an idea.

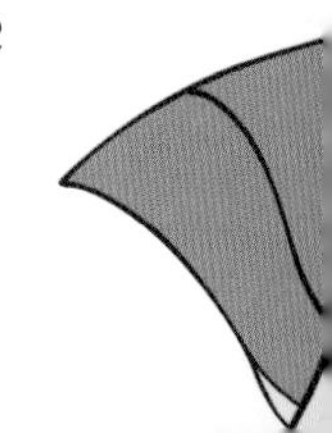

In the morning, he gathered Tigger's friends together and said, "Let's pretend to be Tigger's family and write him a letter to cheer him up."

So they told Owl what to say, and he scribbled a note. It was a fine letter.

It was cold and wintry next day, but Tigger went round to all his friends, waving his letter. "Look!" he cried. "A letter from my own Tigger family!"

They were all pleased their letter had made Tigger so happy. But then he said, "And guess what, my family are coming to visit me – tomorrow!"

His friends knew that wasn't in their letter. Roo wanted to tell Tigger the truth, but he didn't want to make Tigger sad.

Then Roo had another idea. "We'll paint Tigger stripes on ourselves and dress up, then he'll think *we're* his family!"

So that's what they did.

It snowed the next day. And Tigger's friends walked to his house that night dressed in stripes and masks.

Tigger smiled when he saw them. "Hey, let's do some bouncin'," he cried.

They all started bouncing. Then Roo tried the Whoop-de-Dooper Bounce, but he tripped, and his mask fell off. Tigger recognised Roo straightaway. Tigger looked round at the others. "I see, it was all a big joke," he said unhappily.

Then he turned and went out into the cold night. "There's a real Tigger family out there," he said, "and I'm going to find 'em. T-T-F-E – Ta-Ta-For-Ever!"

The next morning, Roo was very upset. He asked Pooh if he would help to find Tigger and bring him home.

Pooh agreed, and all Tigger's friends set off through the snow to look for him.

In another part of the Wood, Tigger had found a magnificent tree. "My family tree! Hello, Tigger family, are you there?" he called excitedly. But there was no reply. A moment later, the wind blew his family letter away.

Tigger's shoulders drooped. Now he really was alone.

But Tigger wasn't alone at all. The letter blew straight to where Roo was, with Pooh, Piglet, Rabbit and Eeyore.

Roo knew Tigger would not be far away from his family letter. The friends all shouted his name, but Tigger couldn't hear. He was high up in the tree, feeling miserable.

Suddenly there was a loud rumbling noise and Tigger jumped down. “Hey, what’re you doing here?” he cried, amazed to see his friends.

Before anyone could answer, they saw a huge pile of snow heading straight for them! Tigger picked up his friends, and bounced them to safety in the tree.

Then just when everything seemed fine, Tigger was swept away in the snow. Horrified, Roo bounced after his friend with a wonderful Whoop-de-Dooper Bounce.

"That was a real Tigger bounce!" said Tigger when they were both safe.

Tigger realised that his real family had been with him all along. As soon as they were home, he gave them a great party, with presents for everyone.

Roo got the best present – Tigger's locket. Inside there was a family picture of all of them.

And so they were together once more – as they will always be – as a family in the Hundred Acre Wood.